# What is a CROCODILE'S FAVOURITE Thing?

This book is dedicated to my love Zinia
– will you marry me?

WHAT IS A CROCODILE'S FAVOURITE THING?
A JONATHAN CAPE BOOK  978 1 780 08022 2

Published in Great Britain by Jonathan Cape, an imprint of Random House Children's Publishers UK
A Random House Group Company
This edition published 2013

1 3 5 7 9 10 8 6 4 2

Copyright © Ben Hawkes, 2013 The right of Ben Hawkes to be identified as the author and illustrator
of this work has been asserted in accordance with the Copyright, Designs and Patents Act 1988.
All rights reserved. RANDOM HOUSE CHILDREN'S PUBLISHERS UK
61 – 63 Uxbridge Road, London, W5 5SA

www.randomhouse.co.uk
www.randomhousechildrens.co.uk

Addresses for companies within The Random House Group Limited can be found at:
www.randomhouse.co.uk/offices.htm
THE RANDOM HOUSE GROUP Limited Reg. No. 954009
A CIP catalogue record for this book is available from the British Library
Printed in China

MIX
Paper from
responsible sources
FSC® C020056

The Random House Group Limited supports the Forest Stewardship Council (FSC®), the leading international
forest certification organization. Our books carrying the FSC label are printed on FSC®-certified paper.
FSC is the only forest certification scheme endorsed by the leading environmental organizations, including
Greenpeace. Our paper procurement policy can be found at www.randomhouse.co.uk/environment.

# What is a CROCODILE'S FAVOURITE Thing?

## WARNING!
THIS IS A VERY SILLY BOOK,
READING THIS BOOK MAY CAUSE SILLINESS,
MORE SILLINESS AND, IN SOME CASES,
YOUR BOTTOM MAY DROP OFF.

**Ben Hawkes**

Jonathan Cape · London

I wonder, do you know what is a crocodile's favourite thing?

# Is it racing a car that looks like a sausage?

Or is it being as *stinky* as old cheese?

NO!

Is it doing ballet

Or is it wearing pyjamas
made from bananas?

NO!

I don't think **that** is his favourite thing.

So I wonder, can **you** tell what **is** a crocodile's favourite thing?

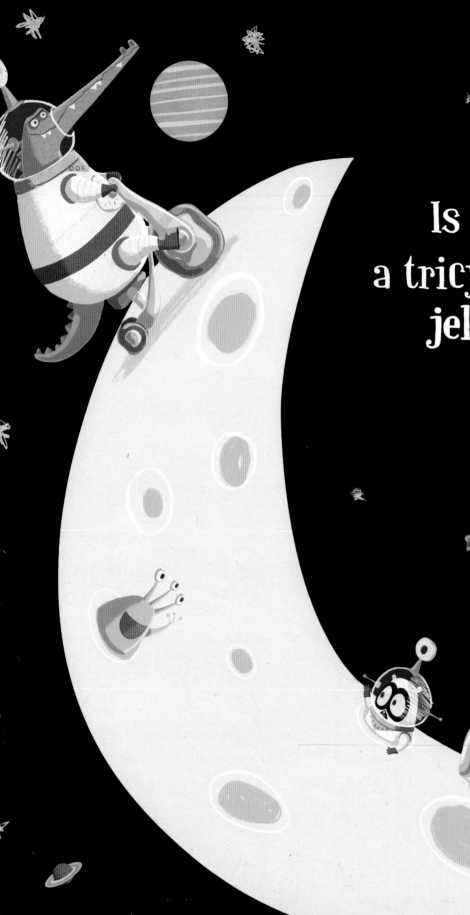

Is it riding
a tricycle made of
jelly on the
moon?

Or is it having a bath
full of **mud** and **worms?**

NO!

Is it taming a very grumpy lion at the circus?

# NO!

**That's** not a crocodile's favourite thing!

I **wonder**, can you guess
just what **is** a crocodile's
favourite thing?

Is it squashing tomatoes with his big green bottom?

Or is it being a **clown** at a little girl's party?

Is it playing hide-and-seek

with a huge, massive **elephant?**

Is it . . .

. . . eating a **dirty** pants sandwich?

NO!

. . . finding his hat is full of custard?

NO!

. . . stuffing a carrot right up his nose?

NO!

Or is it watering
a *lovely* big flower?

# NO!
## Of course not, silly!

I'll tell you what a crocodile's favourite thing is . . .

# DINNER
# TIME!

# OUCH!